Treasures in the Winter Vault

Debbie Bertram & Lisa Detanna

illustrated by
Kevin Greene

Headline Kids
an imprint of Headline Books, Inc.
Terra Alta, WV

Treasures in the Winter Vault

by Debbie Bertram & Lisa Detanna
illustrated by Kevin Greene

copyright ©2015 Debbie Bertram & Lisa Detanna

To order additional copies of this book, or for book publishing information, or to contact the author:

Headline Kids
P. O. Box 52
Terra Alta, WV 26764

Tel: 800-570-5951
Email: mybook@headlinebooks.com
www.headlinebooks.com
www.headlinekids.com

Published by Headline Books
Headline Kids is an imprint of Headline Books

Lisa Detanna
BEVERLY HILLS 9595 Wilshire Blvd., Suite 300 // Beverly Hills, CA 90212
LOS ANGELES 444 South Flower St., Suite 3870 // Los Angeles, CA 90071
www.raymondjames.com/globalwealthsolutionsgroup
T: 310.285.4506 // 888-900-1311 // F: 213.327.1030

ISBN 9781882658220 (hardcover)
ISBN 9781882658237 (paperback)

Library of Congress Control Number: 2014957103

PRINTED IN THE UNITED STATES OF AMERICA

Bobby cried into his pillow. He lifted his head, talking to the stuffed animals on his bed.

"Why CAN'T I have a new tablet?" he cried. I want a tablet! Everyone at school has one but ME! I want one, too! It's not fair!"

Bobby continued to cry. "Not fair! Not fair!"

There was a soft knock at his door. He ignored it.

"Bobby? It's Grandma and Grandpa. Your mom and dad said you were in your room. May we come in?"

Bobby sniffled. "I guess," he mumbled.

They came into Bobby's bedroom. Grandma sat down beside Bobby on the bed. Grandpa sat down in the squishy bean bag chair.

"We came to have dinner with all of you this evening," Grandma said. "And Mom and Dad said you were up here in your room and very upset."

"Do you want to tell us what's wrong?" asked Grandpa.

Bobby sat up on his bed, holding his favorite stuffed bear.

He sniffled and said, "I asked Mom and Dad if I could have a tablet and they said, NO! Everyone has one but me. It's not fair!"

Grandpa asked, "Do you have any money saved to buy one, Bobby?"

"Well, no," he answered. "I spent all of my money on comic books and candy."

Grandpa said, "When I was a young boy, if I wanted something, I had to save up my allowance. I did a lot of extra chores and—"

"Never mind all of that right now," Grandma interrupted. "Let me tell you a story, Bobby. This is a story that my grandma told me when I was a little girl."

Bobby turned over on his back, scrunching his pillow underneath his head.

Grandma began:

All of the squirrels played together. They chased each other up and down the trees all day long. Up, down, up, down and all around the branches at top speed!

They collected all kinds of different nuts while they played. They cracked them open, tossed them into their mouths and played some more.

An elephant watched the squirrels playing from a nearby oak tree. This elephant loved to dance. She did a little ballet, then a little tap dance and then a little hip-hop. She did the tango and then a little cha-cha. She took a bow. The squirrels applauded. "Bravo!"

9

And the squirrels dashed by, in between their games, tossing nuts into the dancing elephant's welcoming mouth. They tumbled onto her trunk with their bushy tails. Everyone was enjoying the warm, sunny day.

Bobby closed his eyes and smiled.

Grandma continued:

One afternoon, Sergeant Squirrel called everyone together for an important meeting. "Attention!" his voice boomed, "Listen well, one and all. Playtime is over! All of us have enjoyed a wonderful spring and a happy, carefree summer, but now it is time to get to work. Everyone must do their share to gather nuts for the winter and deliver them to our Winter Vault!

"What's a Winter Vault, Grandma?" Bobby asked.

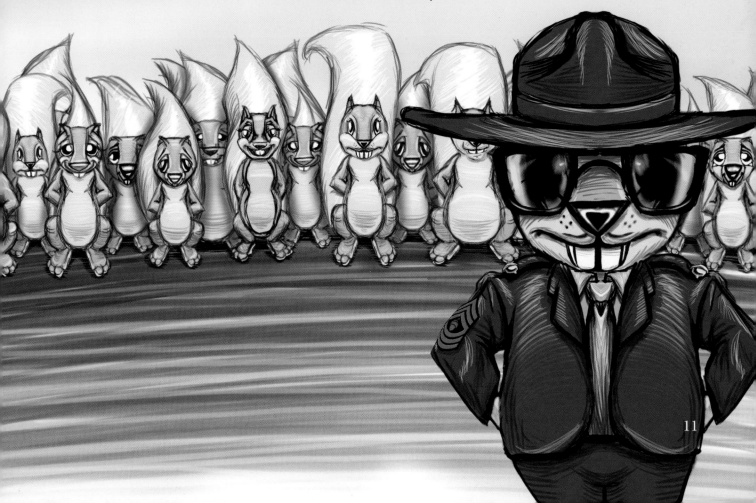

Grandma explained, "A Winter Vault is the place for all of the squirrels to safely hide their nuts so they will be ready and waiting when winter arrives."

"And what about the elephant?" asked Bobby, "Did she help?"

Well, she had promised the squirrels she would help them since she could carry SO much more than all of the squirrels could. But every time she thought about collecting nuts, she forgot about helping and started to dance. She tap, tap tapped and stood up as high as she could on her toes, forgetting all about helping the squirrels.

So, the squirrels filled boxes with nuts. They filled wheelbarrows and wagons. They filled everything they could find. They gathered and gathered and delivered nut after nut to their Winter Vault.

"That was a good idea," said Bobby.

Grandma continued:

And as the days grew cooler and the sun set earlier the nuts became scarce and there were none left to eat. There were no leaves on the trees. The squirrels were ready to move into their Winter Vault. The elephant continued to dance and dance. She tapped her left foot, then her right foot and spun around again and again.

"Just a little good-bye dance for all of you lovely squirrels," she said, as she did a perfect pirouette.

"You better think about the cold winter days ahead," warned Sergeant Squirrel. And the elephant replied, "Oh, there's plenty of time left before it will be cold." And she finished her dance with a curtsy.

And soon, just as Sergeant Squirrel
had warned, it became very, very cold.
"Oh, no!" Bobby said.

As the squirrels settled in to their warm, cozy Winter Vault, the elephant continued to dance...but her dancing was slowing down. She was cold. And she was hungry. She shivered. B-r-r-r.

"She should have thought about that, Grandma," Bobby frowned.

Grandma continued:

First she went down to the river to get a drink, but the water was frozen. She tried to dance her way back, but her feet were too cold. She moved slowly...very slowly. And by the time she returned to the squirrels' Winter Vault, she had icicles dripping from her trunk and snow between her toes.

And then...all two tons of that poor, freezing, starving elephant... all 4,000 pounds of her...collapsed right there...to the ground...and she fell so hard the earth shook!

Bobby grabbed his pillow, "Oh, no!"

"Oh, yes!" Grandma said, "and the elephant lay there on the ground, covered with ice and snow."

Until...

Baby Squirrel poked his little head out. He gasped when he saw the elephant lying there! He ran inside to get help.

And every squirrel, every single one of them, came out to help...and that was a lot of squirrels! After all, how many squirrels do you think it takes to pick up an elephant?"

Bobby just shook his head.

They carried the elephant inside. She was not moving. The squirrels took their teeny-tiny spoons and started feeding her little squirrel spoonfuls of hot-nut stew. Spoonful after spoonful. And...after six thousand spoonfuls of hot-nut stew, the elephant finally began to warm up inside. She opened one eye...and then the other. She raised her trunk and warmly hugged all of the squirrels. And then she smiled her biggest, happiest, toothiest elephant grin!

"Hooray!" All of the squirrels cheered!

"Did they live happily ever after, Grandma?"
Grandma smiled and continued:
"When the next summer was coming to an end and fall was just around the corner, it was time for the squirrels to collect nuts again for their Winter Vault. While they were working hard collecting their winter nuts, the elephant danced. She did a little hip-hop, a little samba and a little cha-cha-cha...and then, all of sudden, she stopped! And she stood still.

All of the squirrels stopped nut collecting. They watched the elephant to see what dance she was going to do next. But she did not dance at all.

The elephant bent all the way down. She slowly got up and stood as tall as she could. She reached high into the sky with her long trunk. And when she brought her trunk down, she started filling it with nuts...hundreds of them, thousands of them! It looked like a vacuum-cleaner, sucking up nut after nut!

And she tap-danced right over to the squirrels' Winter Vault and blew! She blew those nuts right out of her trunk! And just like that, lickety-split, all of the squirrels had enough nuts in their Winter Vault to keep them in nuts all winter...with some left over!

"Wow, Grandma!" Bobby laughed. "I love that story! I guess that elephant learned her lesson about being prepared."

"Yup!" Grandpa answered.

"Maybe next time if I want something that is important to me, like a tablet, I will be more prepared, too. Is that what you were trying to tell me?"

"Yup!" Grandma and Grandpa answered. And Grandpa walked over to Bobby's piggy bank and dropped some coins in. "Plink-Plunk!"

Grandpa winked at Grandma, and she smiled back at him.

31

Bobby jumped off the bed and ran over to hug Grandma and Grandpa.

And while he was hugging them, he heard his mother calling from downstairs, "Dinner's ready!"